BUTTERMILK

Written By
STEPHEN COSGROVE

Illustrated By
ROBIN JAMES

Rourke Enterprises, Inc.
Vero Beach, FL 32964

A Serendipity™ Book

© 1986 Rourke Enterprises, Inc.
© 1986 Price/Stern/Sloan Publishers, Inc.

Library of Congress Cataloging in Publication Data

Cosgrove, Stephen.
  Buttermilk.

  "A Serendipity book."
  Summary: Buttermilk the bunny thinks she sees
scary monsters while trying to find her way home
after dark, but the light of day puts things in
a different perspective.
  [1. Rabbits—Fiction.   2. Night—Fiction.
3. Fear—Fiction.   4. Monsters—Fiction]   I. James,
Robin, ill.   II. Title.
PZ7.C8187BV   1986   [Fic]   86-15590
ISBN 0-86592-241-1

Dedicated to my loving Shaerie, who always manages to see beyond the shadows of the monsters of my mind.

Stephen

There was a land — a beautiful land of wispy fog and setting suns. A land filled with gentle unfulfilled dreams and streams flowing with wishes and wants. For this was the land of Chimera, a place where your dreams go when you fall asleep.

There lived in the land of Chimera many delightful creatures. But none were so delightful as the bunnies, whose fur was as fluffy as dandelion down and whose eyes shone like shiny black lumps of coal. Their noses twitched at the slightest breeze as they sniffed about looking for friend or foe, and when they felt that it was safe they would hop on large thumping feet down paths covered in needles from the trees called Velvet Pines.

One such bunny of Chimera was a delightful creature with fur the color of cream sprinkled with light, bright golden splotches. Seen in the proper light her fur reminded one of buttermilk and that is what she was called: Buttermilk.

Late one day, as the sun was setting low and the shadows were getting longer, Buttermilk realized that she had wandered far away from her home. With a nervous look from side to side, she began hopping home while remembering all the spooky stories the older bunnies had always told of ghosts and goblins. It seemed that the faster she hopped the longer the shadows became until she found herself in a very dark, scary night. Buttermilk's fuzzy pouf of a tail quivered in fear as she hopped faster and faster through what her mind had made into a very frightening forest.

She had just hopped around a corner of the path, nervously looking over her shoulder at what she knew must be a ghost or a goblin, when right before her stood the most ferocious dragon she had ever seen. Well, it was also the only dragon she had ever seen, but scary just the same. The dragon stood at least nine feet tall with scales of green and yellow plated armor that fluttered as the dragon breathed. Its wings were furled like giant sails as it towered above the frightened bunny. Suddenly, the terrible wings began to move, making the most terrifying sound.

"Get moving, feet! Just run!" Buttermilk stuttered as her feet began to pound against the ground, and run she did like she had never run before.

Always looking behind her, Buttermilk hopped and hopped down the velvety path in the ever-deepening darkness. She had just hopped over a rotting log when she saw before her a more-than-monstrous bear. The bear, with hulking shoulders and long knife-like teeth, sat hunched at the edge of the path just waiting for an unsuspecting, bungling bunny like Buttermilk to come along. The bear's teeth began to chatter in anticipation of a busy, bushy, bundle of baby bunny breakfast.

"Come on feet, make motion!" she said as her legs, thumping like two pumping pistons, kicked up pine needles as she raced down the path.

She was really moving now, and nothing would have stopped her escape from the forest to her den — except for the banshee. What a horrible, horrible sight: red glowing eyes and the fluttering sound of its horrible creaking limbs. Its hideous head swiveled from side to side looking for a bunny to munch on as it moaned, "Ooooh! Oooh!"

"Feet, just keep on moving, don't wait for me! Save yourself!" Buttermilk panted through chattering teeth. Then, running faster than fast, her feet nearly outran her up the forest path.

With her heart pounding in her ears, Buttermilk dashed through the thicket and hopped down the hole that was her home. She skittered through twisted, darkened tunnels filled with hanging roots and dived with relief into her bed. She pulled the quilt of soft, woven grasses up over her head and tried to get rid of all the fear she felt. She scrunched her face into pillows filled with pollen and tried so hard to fall asleep, but it was to no avail. Buttermilk could still hear the rustling of the monsters in the forest outside.

She had been shaking in her bed for only a few minutes when she heard the shuffling feet in the tunnel of her den. "Screep! Thunk! Screep! Thunk!" The horrible sound of the monsters' footsteps echoed in the hall.

"Buttermilk? Are you okay?" asked her father in his low, foggy voice. "We heard you come in, but you didn't stop for supper or say goodnight to your mother and me."

Buttermilk rushed from her bed and into the big furry arms of her father's embrace. "Oh, Poppa!" she cried. "They were horrible, all the monsters of the shadows and the night. There was a banshee and a bear and a dragon of fright."

"Don't be afraid," gently crooned her father as he swept her up into his arms. "Tomorrow in the light we'll find your monsters, but for now, my little bundle of bunny, you must close your eyes and go to sleep." With that, he walked and rocked his daughter until she fell asleep.

Bright and early, the very next morning, as the dew was still dripping, Buttermilk and her father hopped down the path and retraced her terrible flight of the night before. Floppy step by floppy step they moved up the path until they came to the place where Buttermilk had seen the banshee. They looked and looked and listened too for the creaking limbs and the cry, "Ooooohhh! Oooohh!" But all they found was a baby barn owl who cried softly out, "Whooo? Whooo?"

"See," said her father, "when you find your nighttime monsters in the light they aren't filled with fear or fright."

Buttermilk scrunched up her nose and said, "Well, maybe the banshee was just an owl, but just wait until I show you the hulking bear." And off they hopped down the path in the morning mist.

They rounded the path to the spot where the bear had been the night before, but there was no bear there. Instead, there was an overgrown hump of a stump with mushrooms growing in great profusion. "A busy, bushy, bundle of baby bunny breakfast indeed," chuckled her father.

"But Poppa," she said, "I heard his teeth chattering in anticipation." Then, as if by cue, a tiny striped chipmunk appeared and chittered and chattered at the two of them.

"Well," giggled Buttermilk, "maybe the banshee was an owl and the bear was a stump, but just wait until I show you the most monstrous of dragons!" And so she hopped ahead, nervously retracing her steps with her father shuffling behind.

They hipped and hopped until they came to the place where Buttermilk had been attacked by the most monstrous dragon. But instead of a dragon, they found a beautiful weeping willow tree dripping with bright green leaves and filled with golden butterflies that danced in the wind. Flittering and fluttering amidst the butterflies was a flock of mountain canaries who chirped and sang in their morning's delight.

"Gee, Poppa, I feel so dumb!' said a humbled Buttermilk as she twisted and turned her foot in the path. "I shouldn't have been so scared."

"No," said her father in the gentlest of ways, "don't feel dumb. For everything seems a little darker and scarier at night, but in the daytime, the light is bright and shoos away all of your worst fears." With that, he wiped away all her tears and arm in arm they hopped back to their burrow in the woods.

Behind them, the weeping willow whispered in the wind, and if you looked very closely, you would have seen a baby dragon hiding beneath it, looking at you and me.

REMEMBER, AT NIGHTTIME
WITHIN SHADOWS DEEP,
THERE AREN'T ANY MONSTERS
CLOSE YOUR EYES, GO TO SLEEP